Quantum Lace

~ BOOK ONE ~

Quantum Lace

Book One

Dedicated to my aunt with whom I am so blessed to have been recently reconnected ~ the loving, intelligent, beautiful and inspiring **Carol Morgan** ~ through whose example I am learning what it feels like to have a 'family'.

Thank you and I hope you enjoy the book...

"Sit down before fact like a little child and be prepared to give up every preconceived notion, follow humbly wherever and to whatever abyss Nature leads, or you shall learn nothing."

Thomas Henry Huxley
(4 May, 1825 - 29 June 1895)

As you read this book, may you follow Huxley's words, not his example (that's another story!), and be prepared to give up every preconceived notion of what you thought was impossible.

As Audrey Hepburn once said, "Nothing is *impossible*, the word itself says 'I'm possible'!"

Once upon a time... Sounds like a simple enough way to start a story – and particularly a story about time travel, but what does it mean, 'once upon a time'? What *is* time?

Clocks can tell us what time it is, but they cannot tell us <u>what time is</u>!

In fact, we can only define time using terms that are related to time. One definition states time is "defined by its measurement". Even the most un-educated will agree there is something very circular in that reasoning and lacking in that definition.

The story of time travel you are about to read, while a work of fiction, is largely based on real science, real people and real events. Where fact leaves off and fiction begins is for you to decide.

Do a search on just about anything in this book and make up your own mind what is 'real'.

For instance, Morgan Robertson really did publish a book on the sinking of an 'unsinkable ship' that hit an iceberg fourteen years before Titanic; the edition of "The Time Machine" published by Holt, really did misspell Wells' name as H.S. Wells and his address listed on the letter sent to Bridgit, was Wells' actual address at the time; Lord Brassey really did go off to Australia to become Governor of Victoria and his first wife did die on board the 'Sunbeam'; the quotes from Tesla's presentation are actually verbatim of the words he uttered in 1892; and the quantum physics mentioned is all real scientific fact as we know it today...

In this first book of the *Quantum Lace* series, Lady Bridgit Darnell's life in 1895 in England is interrupted with what she initially thought was merely a strange dream – a dream in which she meets present-day Markus in South Carolina who tells her not only that quantum physics has shown time-travel is possible, but he outlines how he himself has already been able to travel through time.

Awaking back in what she recognizes as her own time and place, Bridgit is convinced the vision must have been a fantasy of her own making until an event occurs that proves the dream was in fact *real*, and the ripple effect of which alters Bridgit's life forever...

Table of Contents

"I am home," Bridgit mumbled sleepily to herself as she slowly opened her eyes and carefully looked around her familiar bedroom, reflecting on the events of the past several hours, or was it just a few minutes?

Some dreams are simply a jumbled mish-mash of the day's comings and goings. This had not been one of those dreams... Nor was it a problem-solving dream where one has visions of cryptic clues that help alleviate a challenging situation.

To be completely honest, this did not feel to Bridgit as though it was a dream at all, but yet...

Her thoughts were interrupted by Dixon who came in to open the curtains, releasing a bright display of dust particles dancing in the shard of daylight that came streaming into the room.

"Are you well this morning, Miss?" asked the short, slightly plump but very agile Dixon with a caring tone but displaying a lack of any interest in not only the answer, but indeed whether or not an answer was even given. She was too intent going about her morning chores, confident that if Miss had been other than well, she would already know about it.

Although originally hired as lady's maid to Lady Bridgit Darnell, when the housekeeper, Mrs. Capwell, left to move to Brighton with her son, Dixon took charge of the household with such military precision that it was not deemed necessary to hire a replacement.

With the precision of a well-rehearsed soldier, the be-spectacled, grey-haired Dixon went from one activity to the next, all the while commenting in great detail on the unusually fine weather and excess of sunshine that May of 1895 in Warrior Square had bestowed upon them.

"You'll be wanting to take this shawl with you down to the shore, Miss. It may be bright and sunny out theres abouts, but it is still mighty chilly and you don't want to catch cold. I'll be back up in ten minutes to help you dress. I've laid out the blue for today. Mrs. Patterson still hasn't fixed that rip you put in the hem of your brown one when you caught it the other day. I keep telling her 'we ain't made of clothes, you know' and all I gets is 'I'll see to it...' See to it my foot. That woman would take seven minutes to boil a three-minute egg, she would..."

Normally not the role of the cook to mend a hem, but Mrs. Patterson took extra pride in her sewing ability and when she once criticized Dixon for a crooked seam, it was decided in order to avert domestic warfare, that in the future all manner of things to do with fabric and thread would be the domain of Mrs. Patterson.

Only Bridgit and her father were in residence and, despite their social position entertaining was something they did rarely, so aside from Dixon and Mrs. Patterson, the remainder of the household staff consisted only of Mr. Chapman the butler; Perkins the valet; Annie, who took on both responsibilities of kitchen maid and general under-housemaid duties; and the tasks of houseboy fell to Perkins' nephew, Rodney.

There was one other addition to the household staff - the rather now aged French chef, Monsieur Dubois who had worked for Sir Frank Darnell decades ago and, when Sir Frank discovered the man was now homeless and penniless because he was infirm and no longer able to run a large kitchen, had hired him to join the staff at their home in Warrior Square as chef - however, the only time Monsieur was required to cook was if either Sir Frank or Lady Bridgit felt in the mood for something in particular – the rest of Monsieur's days were spent reading and reminiscing.

As she had completed her immediate chores and not waiting for a response from her mistress, Dixon left the room, closing the door behind her and leaving Bridgit again to her thoughts.

Yesterday had been quite an ordinary day, yesterday evening equally so. Bridgit retired as usual and went to sleep, but as she began to dream, that was where normal ended.

She imagined she was seated in a booth in a large restaurant overlooking a harbour. Massive arched windows gave her an almost one-hundred-eighty-degree vista, but something was odd. The boats were all white in colour and almost to a vessel they were absent of any masts...

"How strange," Bridgit remarked supposedly to herself but obviously loud enough that a young woman standing near her said, "I'm sorry? I didn't hear you. What would you like to order?"

"Oh, ah... tea would be lovely, thank you."

"Is that all?" asked the server in an accent that was completely unfamiliar to Bridgit. Since 'talkies' were many years away in Bridgit's reality, the only people in 1895 England who would have heard an American accent were those who had either travelled abroad or had met someone originally from America – Bridgit had done neither.

"Yes, thank you," replied Bridgit feeling rather confused. The young woman was dressed in tight black trousers and a form-fitting shirt with short sleeves, all of which showed off her figure in a way that caused Bridgit to stare. If only she had looked at her own apparel, Bridgit would have been startled to discovered she was wearing something similar, although a skirt not pants and not quite so form-fitting.

"Well, if you want anything else, I'll leave the menu here with you," said the server as she walked off with her white-soled shoes squeaking on the floor as she left.

Looking down at the large document as it sat on the solid, heavy wooden table, on the cover Bridgit read the name of the restaurant and below it the location – Charleston, South Carolina.

South Carolina?

Suddenly even more aware of her surroundings, Bridgit's eyes darted about the room, her ears picking up on sounds and conversations.

It was not just the young woman who was dressed oddly. The entire establishment was full of people whose dress, manner and even conversation were beyond comprehension.

"Thank goodness you're still here!" exclaimed a man in his early thirties as he hurriedly sat down in the booth opposite Bridgit.

"Excuse me?" remarked a startled Bridgit, but the man was undeterred.

"I did it, Bridge!" he continued. "I did it!" he exclaimed again as he excitedly reached across the table and took both Bridgit's hands in his, quickly squeezing them and letting them go.

"How dare you!" exclaimed Bridgit but to her surprise, Markus didn't seem at all perturbed by her response.

Bridgit was wide-eyed and totally aghast at the cheek of this man. Thinking he must surely come to his senses, apologize and remove himself, Bridgit waited in silence, eyeing him with bewilderment and suspicion.

"I know, I know – I should have been in touch and I'm sure you've been worried, so I'm sorry for that, but Bridge!" He paused very briefly, then continued. "Wow, where to begin," Markus said with a sigh, totally oblivious to Bridgit's horror as he sat back against the bench seat, allowing his manic enthusiasm to dissipate slightly and eventually looked down searchingly at the table in a vain hope he would somehow see the starting point for his explanation in the grains of the wood, unaware of Bridgit's perplexed glare.

The moment was interrupted by the waitress who returned with Bridgit's order and placed a glass of iced tea on the table.

"What is this?" asked Bridgit who was expecting a very English pot, cup and saucer.

"Tea," replied the waitress. "You'll find sugar and sweeteners at the end of the table," as she pointed to a container of blue, pink and white small paper satchels.

Bridgit reluctantly took a sip. It looked and tasted like black tea but why on earth was it cold?

The waitress asked the man now sitting opposite Bridgit in the booth what he would like to select from the menu.

"Nothing yet, but I'll wave you down when I'm ready to order," he said very obviously wanted to get rid of the server as soon as possible.

Bridgit felt a flood of emotions course through her. Enraged at the impertinence of this man... Curiosity at the bizarre nature of his actions, her cold beverage, and of essentially everything within sight and earshot... and a mild sense of fear that she that she was seemingly trapped in a bizarre play from which she knew not how to leave.

"OK, well, I guess it all started when I found out that Dmitri Mendeleev, you know, the guy who came up with the periodic table of elements." The fact that this man seemed to know her was one thing – he might simply have made an error and thought she was someone else... But he called her "Bridge"! ...and then there was the fact that everyone and everything around her was peculiar beyond measure...

"Where am I?" Bridgit wondered apprehensively to herself but didn't venture to say aloud.

At a loss for any other course of action and, if she were completely honest, more than a little intrigued enough to learn more, Bridgit nodded and motioned for the man to continue. "When I learned that he discovered the whole periodic table in a dream – a dream! – the entire periodic table, in a dream! – that started me thinking..." Markus trailed off in thought.

Bridgit didn't know what to do other than to sit patiently and await the continuation.

Markus looked at Bridgit intently and said, "It's like it all came together, Bridge. Quantum physics, holographic universes, spirituality... Everything I have read and studied by people like Dr. Fred Alan Wolf – you know him, Dr. Quantum – and Neville Goddard, and the research done by... What's that Reverend man's name? I can never remember it."

Bridgit shrugged. "Fanthorpe, that's it. Reverend Lionel Fanthorpe," he continued. "Even the work of people like Giorgio Tsoukalos or however you say his name – you know, the guy with the crazy hair – and Gene Roddenberry... They might seem totally unrelated, but they are not – they all came together in that moment and," he lowered the volume of his voice but not his intensity, "I knew that the piece I had been missing was to time travel in a *dream* when all resistance has stopped!" He emphasized the word with such veracity and passion that even though she was perplexed by this man and her current surroundings, her instinct was to trust him and allow him to continue.

As he looked at her face, Markus could see Bridgit was confused but there was an directness in her eyes that gave him the confidence she would give him a fair hearing, even though he knew what he was saying sounded crazy, even to him.

"Let's start with some basics," he began. "You know that for some time we thought that Steven Hawking was right when he said nothing, not even information, could escape a black hole?"

Bridgit had no notion of what he was talking about but decided it was best to just nod and allow him to resume his explanation.

"When Leonard Susskind proved that Stephen Hawking was wrong – that information is not obliterated in a black hole but rather that information cannot ever be destroyed, it felt as though I had somehow been given permission to continue with my quest. Instinctively I *knew* that Hawking's theory didn't fit with what I believed, but I had no way of challenging it. Thankfully, Susskind did that for me! I love him for that!" he chuckled as though the only one in on a private joke.

"Well, since we now know that information cannot be destroyed, that means that *every* thought anyone has ever had, *every* dream, *every* experience... It's all still available – right back to the beginning of time."

Bridgit again nodded and although she didn't understand the rest of what he was saying, that element at least made sense.

"It is called the Unitarity Principle," he continued, "and it says that information can never be lost – it is always there, even if it's not visible. The only challenge we have is being able to tap into it, and that's where personal resonance comes in."

"Personal what?" asked Bridgit, now too far out of her depth so simply nod obligingly and follow along.

"There was a psychologist called Anderson who proposed that we *can* tap into all that information, but only if we have some type of connection to it – a personal resonance. Kinda like a vibrating tuning fork will resonate with another tuning fork *only* if the second tuning fork is the same frequency as the first – or in other words, the vibrational frequencies match."

Since Bridgit had learned of the musical vibration principle in her formative studies, she was at least following along in this part of the conversation, but did not understand how it applied to whatever the man opposite was attempting to convey.

He continued, "For instance, if you have a tuning fork tuned to middle C and then you tap it on the table and stand it on its end so it sings, any other tuning forks near it that are also tuned to middle C will also start to sing, but a tuning fork tuned to A for instance, will not."

Markus looked intently at Bridgit to see if she was following. "Go on," she said hesitantly.

"Sound waves are *amazing!*" enthused Markus. "I mean in 2007 scientists showed that sound pulses can travel faster than light – imagine that, faster than light! – and then in 2008 it was discovered that if you are able to determine the resonance or vibrational frequency of a virus, you can destroy it using that resonance – and in 2015 they even built a machine that was able to levitate objects using nothing but sound waves! Or think about the invention by a guy called Peter Davey that is able to boil water in seconds using only sound waves!" Markus was on a roll and Bridgit was sure she must have misheard him – "2015?"

"Don't you get it? They are central to being able to travel through time," he said, misunderstanding her expression of confusion. "We can't simply bounce around aimlessly in time – we need to have some sort of connection to where we are going. We need to match the vibrational frequency, just like they did with the virus – to have a personal resonance, just like the tuning forks." He paused, then smirked, "Hmmmm, or perhaps that should be *when* we are going," again, he laughed to himself. Bridgit was not amused.

Noting her scornful look and feeling like a chastised schoolboy, Markus composed himself and resumed, "Part of the preparation for time travel is to have some vibrational connection to where you want to go," he continued. "Einstein said, 'Everything in life is vibration' and everything has its own vibrational frequency, whether it is a rat, a rock or this table," he said as he patted his hand down on the sturdy chunk of wood.

"Einstein?" asked Bridgit tentatively.

"What?" questioned Markus looking at her with raised eyebrows. He didn't realize it would still be another ten years in Bridgit's time before Einstein's famous works were published.

"Who is Einstein?" she replied in an almost staccato fashion.

After a momentary pause, Markus chuckled aloud. "OK, funny, Miss Smarty Pants. Trying to throw me off." He sat back again, grinned, and then again leaned forward saying, "Look, Bridge, I know this sounds crazy, but I have already done it – and I have proof that it works..."

Bridgit didn't understand why he mocked her question, but decided to again simply be quiet, nod, and follow along as best she could.

"OK, I will get back to the resonance and objects in a minute. The other thing you need to know is how reality is created." He looked at her for some indication that she was ready to proceed but getting only a bewildered stare he decided to continue regardless.

"With every choice and decision we make, with every event in our life that could go a variety of different directions, a parallel universe branches off... Now, just stick with me – I'll explain..." he hastily added before Bridgit could interject.

"Back in 1982, a physicist named Alain Aspect proved that either objective reality does not exist – meaning there is no such thing as what we consider the see it, feel it, touch it reality - *or* communication with both the past and the present is possible – and that's not just hypothesis. He proved beyond a shadow of doubt that one of those two options *must* be accepted as fact. I mean, how amazing is that?" He looked at Bridgit whose complexion was now turning significantly pale and peaked.

"Are you ok?" he asked, reaching out for her hand as she slid it slowly back under the table and out of reach.

"Quite," Bridgit replied quietly and a little breathlessly. She had never been a very believable liar. In her mind, she was attempting to put all the pieces together to defy logic and somehow make it make sense, and felt she was holding her own until 'back in 1982'? Surely, she had misheard him. But then again, one look around her confirmed she was no longer in England in 1895.

Feeling he was in too far to back out now, Markus continued.

"Every time you make a decision, you create reality – but up until you make that decision, every possible alternative exists as a potentiality. Look at it this way – say you are considering whether or not to cross the road. There are countless – infinite, really – possibilities. You could choose to cross the road now, you could choose not to cross the road, you could jay-walk, you could walk part way across the road and come back... They are all possibilities *until* you actually make the decision and take the action. Do you follow?"

"Not really, but keep going," replied Bridgit honestly.

"Well, for each of those possible decisions, any that are strong possibilities actually branch off and form another holographic universe, just like this one – but in one universe you have crossed the road and in another you are still where you started."

"Why do only the strong possibilities form another universe?" she asked, still not following, but doing her best.

"Any possibility needs to have enough energy so it can branch into another universe," Markus replied as though this was common knowledge. "Those without enough energy are called 'terminal universes' and cannot survive – and actually, that leads us to an interesting point," Markus continued, now feeling on another roll.

"The way we create reality is primarily through our *focus,* our *emotions* and our *imagination.* When we think of a possible outcome for a situation, the ones to which we give our focused thought, where we vividly and with intense emotion place ourselves *in* the desired outcome in our imagination – those are the possibilities that survive and split off as separate universes – and the strongest is the one into which our consciousness continues – what we would call 'reality'."

Bridgit briefly contemplated a conversation she had with her father many years ago as he was discussing the notion that everything that exists was once a thought – every chair, every building, every piece of art...

"Hugh Everett proposed that everything that is physically possible happens in some branch of the multiverse – and I happen to largely agree with him," continued Markus. "So, if you take that and combine it with Aspect's finding that either objective reality doesn't exist or communication between past and present is possible, just think about what that means in relation to time travel! Not only can we travel back in time, but we can explore just about every possible choice we could have ever made! *...and,*" he said emphatically and enthusiastically, "we can travel to the future simply because our 'now' is part of the future's past! Do you get it?"

At that moment, there was for Bridgit a welcome interruption.

"Hey, Markus! Good to see you, buddy. Y'all going to the game on Saturday?" said a man in his thirties who was taking a seat at the bar but addressing the person sitting opposite Bridgit in the wooden booth.

"Sure! I'll text you. Let's grab a drink afterward," Markus replied.

Bridgit's head was spinning as she took a sip of tea, her shaking fingers almost spilling the contents of the glass.

"Anyway, like I was saying," he continued as he brought his attention back to the table, again lowering his voice slightly. "I've even been able to take care of the paradox that H.G. Wells encounters in his book, 'The Time Machine'," Markus continued.

"Bertie? What does he have to do with this?" Bridgit blurted out, now momentarily feeling on solid ground as she took a deep breath, her confidence on the rise.

"Who?" replied Markus.

"Wells. Herbert Wells. You said you solved the paradox in his time travel story in the New Review."

"The New Review? What on earth are you talking about?" questioned Markus rather confoundedly.

Bridgit and Wells met at Uppark in West Sussex when they were mere teenagers and had remained life-long friends. His mother was housekeeper at the estate and Wells, Bertie to his family and friends, had the run of the place when he would come to visit – in particular, he spent countless hours with the collection of books in the magnificent white and gold saloon with its almost floor to ceiling windows looking out over the estate, and the room in which the two friends first met and often discussed theoretical and philosophical concepts such as travelling through time and space...

Bridgit had just recently read Wells' serialized version of his time machine story in the New Review periodical, but the tale was yet to be published into a book. In fact, the story had been published several times, in several different formats, under several different titles and with several slightly different storylines, but not yet as one cohesive volume.

"Never mind, please continue," she said with a resigned sigh.

Markus tipped his head to the side and down slightly, raised an eyebrow, and gave Bridgit a considered look, but then continued.

"It was funny – they didn't even get his name right when that book was first published, and now it's a classic!" he laughed. Seeing Bridgit was more perplexed than amused, he continued.

"Anyway, the grandfather paradox that you can't change the past by going back and killing your grandfather before your father was born. You see, it's not really a paradox at all because nothing you do changes *that* past - the one where you needed to be born in order to exist to be having this experience in the first place." Bridgit gave him a blank stare.

"The same applies for the chronology tenet Wells put forward," Markus explained, "where you cannot go back in time and change something that would mean you now don't go back in time in the first place. They are all holograms of an infinite number of pasts, all different universes, different realities, if you will. You cannot go back in time in *this* reality," he said as he tapped the table, "but you can explore every other universe - every other decision and alternative where your consciousness hasn't yet been."

Bridgit's head was swimming but not seeing any means of retreat from the situation, and despite her discomfort, actually being quite captivated by the entire fantastical discourse, she encouraged Markus to continue.

"But, like I said," elaborated Markus, "time travel only applies prior to collapsing the wave function, prior to taking action, when all other alternatives are only potentialities - or in other words, once you have made a decision and taken action, and your consciousness has moved forward into that new, branched-off universe, you cannot travel back prior to that point in *that* universe, but you can travel back in an alternate one."

Markus stopped and looked at Bridgit for a signal of how to proceed, or even whether to proceed.

"So, if you believe all this to be true..." Bridgit's question was cut off.

"The question is: Are we sure what we know now is everything there is to know – or even if what we think of as fact, are we sure that we are correct? Or, is it possible there may be things that are in fact real that we are presently ignorant of?" replied Markus, heading off any suggestion that he may be imagining the whole thing.

"For instance, I have always wondered whether Morgan Robertson was a time traveller," said Markus. "The coincidences are just too freaky."

"What do you mean?" Bridgit inquired, not sure she would even understand his answer, but willing to continue further down the rabbit hole.

"Just before 1900 – I think it was around 1897 or 1898 – Morgan Robertson wrote a book called, 'Futility' all about a huge British ocean liner that was considered unsinkable, and that struck an iceberg in the Northern Atlantic, 400 miles from

Newfoundland, around midnight in the month of April. It sank, with most of her passengers drowning because there were not enough life rafts. Sound familiar?" Bridgit had no recall of any such incident but nodded for him to continue.

"More than that, Robertson's ship was called 'Titan'. How's that for weird?" he said as he raised his eyebrows and looked at Bridgit.

"There were only a few minor differences between the real *Titanic* ship and the *Titan* ship in the book - for instance, Robertson said the ship was travelling at 25 knots when she hit the iceberg, and we now know that it was 22.5 knots - which isn't a big difference, but makes me think that Robertson must have been around in 1912 and then went back to the 1890s," he looked briefly out the windows at Charleston Harbour before continuing.

"You see, I figure he must have been around at the time of the real sinking and travelled back to the nineteenth century from there, because that - the 25 knots - was the speed some of the newspapers reported at the time on the incident. But even apart from that, so many other elements are identical to the real *Titanic* - that, remember, didn't sink until 1912 -

more than a dozen *years* after he wrote the book!"

"I would like to think that Robertson went back to write about the *Titanic* as a warning, rather than knowing it would sell more books when the real ship actually sank," Markus continued.

"I mean, think about it." He proceeded in a comic overly-British tone to his Southern accent. "'Hello, chaps – I know I'm from America and I know nothing about shipping, but if y'all build a great big unsinkable ship in the future, it's going to hit an iceberg and sink – so, don't do it, OK?'"

Markus chuckled. "The idea that he could have warned them is ludicrous, so I guess he did the next best thing – he wrote about it hoping they would see the similarities."

Markus looked at Bridgit with a solemnity as he continued, "Either way, history shows we didn't listen. He did give it another shot in 1914 when he wrote about the Japanese attack on Pearl Harbour, but no one listened to that warning, either – well, they didn't in this reality at least," he sighed with a sadness that touched Bridgit's heart. "Maybe in some other reality we didn't needlessly lose all those lives..."

Markus sat looking contemplatively at the table and tracing the grains in the wood with the tip of his finger.

"Reality is more than what you can perceive through your physical senses, Bridge," he expressed, coming out of his reflective trance. Looking directly at Bridgit, he continued, "Every rational person understands that, even if they never think about it. They acknowledge radio waves exist – waves you are not physically aware of. To you, those radio waves are non-existent – you can't feel them or pick them up with your physical senses. Yet, anyone with an inexpensive receiver can pick up – or more precisely, tune into those signals that are all around you."

Bridgit nodded, again finding just enough in his commentary that made sense to her to allow him to continue.

"Time travel is possible, Bridge, but it's like a jigsaw puzzle – you not only have to have all the right pieces, you have to know how to put them together in the right way to bring the picture – the alternate time-travelled reality picture – to life."

Markus continued, "You know, it's amazing, we think that reality is all 'out there' but consider when you go to the movies. Not only are you simply seeing one still image after the next that gives you the *illusion* of reality and movement and travel through time and space, but when you see a scary picture and something happens suddenly, causing you to jump, your heart-rate goes up, your fight-or-flight reaction kicks in – but yet nothing 'out there' has changed at all! You are still sitting safely in your seat, eating your popcorn that is now probably scattered all over the place," he chuckled.

Seeing Bridgit still did not appear to be amused, he asked, "So, it makes you wonder – what *is* reality and how do we know it exists the way we currently believe it to exist? Because 'reality' certainly isn't the scary bogey-man on the screen who is coming to get you right here and right now in this moment in time – he is just a series of still pictures strung together with some words and music – but yet your mind and your body react as though he were real... So, how can we say we know what 'reality' is for sure?"

Bridgit didn't understand much of what Markus said but did recall reading a book by Mary Shelley that had scared her to the point where she lit several extra lamps in her bedroom in hopes they would make her feel safer and to calm her agitated, frightened state – and yes, just as he said, the monster was not *actually* in her bedroom and she was not in any danger. Her reaction was merely to harmless printed ink on a page – hardly life-threatening – but yet what she perceived as her *reality*, her quickened pulse, her heightened senses were all as if the monster was indeed right there with her.

"Interesting," Bridgit said, as she pondered this bizarre, confusing and nonsensical conversation and situation.

Feeling Bridgit was becoming a tad more promisingly engaged in the entire concept, Markus quickly continued while he had positive momentum. "Another crucial element is *dreaming,* like I said at the beginning." Bridgit nodded. "Well, not exactly dreaming as you might imagine it, but rather the dream state." Markus looked at Bridgit for some signal to continue but at least not getting one to stop, he picked up where he left off.

"When we enter the dream state, all resistance ceases and we are able to move about without the constructs that our perceived reality in our waking hours places upon us – or more specifically, when our conscious mind that tells us what we can and can't do, takes a nap. For instance, think of a dream where you were flying," he waited for an acknowledgement from Bridgit.

"Can you fly like a bird in this reality?" he asked.

"Of course not," replied Bridgit, shuffling uncomfortably in her seat.

"Actually, what if you *can*," said Markus with a smirk, "but the reason you don't is that you think it is impossible. Think about it..." he said leaning forward toward Bridgit. "Once upon a time it was thought impossible to sail around the world. Once upon a time it was thought physically impossible to run a four-minute mile. Once upon a time it was thought impossible to put a man on the moon. Now we know they are not only possible, but we have actually done them, all of them, and more."

Bridgit was about to interject but held her tongue, partly because she didn't know what to say and partly because she felt she might be physically sick if she even opened her mouth at this point.

"We also thought that time travel was impossible, but what I've done," he said and then paused... He wasn't sure what it was, but he only just now realized there was something unfamiliar in the manner of his best friend, however dismissing any concern and taking a deep breath he said, "What I've done is to find a way to travel back and forward in time, Bridge, and I thought perhaps together we might even..."

Markus trailed off the sentence – or was it a question? – and looked at Bridgit to gauge her reaction.

Taking a deep breath and releasing it slowly, Bridgit put her fingers to her temples in a futile attempt to stop her head from throbbing so loudly she could barely hear his words.

"What you are saying, if I understand correctly, is that you want to teach *me* how to travel through time?" Bridgit's eyes now fixed on Markus', her fingers still pressed to the sides of her forehead.

"I know you can do it, Bridge," Markus replied enthusiastically and started giving her instruction as though she had already said yes.

"One vitally important thing you have to remember is to make sure your emotional state is in check before you start the process. Remember the tuning forks – like attracts like. You don't want to be feeling all frantic and upset when you begin or you'll find yourself attracting a frantic time and place like a war zone somewhere else in time! Believe me, I've done it," Markus cautioned, "and it ain't pretty."

"That, and you have to follow exactly what I tell you to do, or my research all shows that you won't be able to come back to the same time and place you left," Markus said with an added level of warning and concern.

"OK, do you think you can give it a go?" he almost sounded as though he was a child asking for something special for Christmas. "Please?"

All Bridgit could do was to remove her fingers from her temples, place her hands on the table, let out a sigh of resignation and say, "Proceed."

At that, Markus excitedly straightened in his seat and gushed, "Excellent! OK, the first thing you need to learn is about psychometry – or the personal resonance objects we mentioned that act kind of like Dr. Strange's 'sling ring'. With the object in your hands, you have to focus. Take what you think of as the physical 'real' world in front of you out of focus and instead, visualize and focus on the destination – the time and place you want to go to – in your mind."

As he spoke, he pulled a small silver article from his pocket and placed it on the table.

"Where did you get that?" Bridgit almost screamed with alarm as she reached for her waistband, only to find it bare of any accessories.

The object on the table in front of her was an antique ladies belt hook, the same chatelaine that Bridgit wore every day – the repousse rose chatelaine Bridgit's father had made for her mother as a wedding present and upon which he had hung both the keys to their new home and a silver verge fusee pocket watch that he said would mark with a pleasant ticking sound every moment of the many years they would spend together. It marked but two years before a black satin ribbon was threaded through the loop at the top, tied into a bow and the now silent piece placed in a drawer along with the rest of Lady Mary Darnell's jewellery.

"Answer me!" Bridgit demanded, but as Markus attempted to answer, his attention was diverted as a small device he had placed on the table vibrated and emitted a loud musical sound that jolted Bridgit awake, back in her own room, in her own time and space...

"It has to be here," Bridgit said frantically to herself as she leapt from the bed and raced to the mahogany dressing table. Sure enough, as she opened the drawer in which she kept her mother's jewellery, Bridgit found the silver chatelaine was sitting where she had placed it last night. She breathed a sigh of relief and clutching the small piece in her hand, curled back up in bed, feeling somewhat more secure with the beloved artefact firmly in her grasp and the weight of the covers providing a welcome sense of protection - protection from what, she wasn't sure - until she drifted back off into a light, albeit restless slumber.

Upon waking and being comforted that she was safely tucked up in her own bed, just as Bridgit was again starting to mull over the events from the dream, precisely ten minutes after she left it Dixon re-entered the bed chamber to help Bridgit dress in time to go downstairs for breakfast. Before leaving her room, Bridgit felt her waist for the wayward chatelaine, just to make sure it was exactly where it ought to be and then, reassured, continued on her way.

Sir Frank Darnell was already seated at the table reading the newspaper when his daughter walked into the room.

Peering over the top of the freshly ironed pages, he commented in a soothing, concerned tone, "You look frightfully tired, my dear. Didn't you get any sleep?"

Giving him a kiss on the forehead as she passed absent-mindedly by on her way toward the food, Bridgit replied, "Not really, Papa. I had the most unusual dream..." but she allowed the sentence to go unfinished as she helped herself to the selection Mrs. Patterson had prepared for them.

"Good Lord! Watch where you are going, woman!" declared a tall, well-set man as he collided full-stride with Bridgit, knocking her backwards.

It was a pleasant day in St Leonards-On-Sea with a cool breeze blowing in off the English Channel.

Bridgit had been lost in thought on her stroll along the sea-front when suddenly she remembered her promise to meet with Elizabeth and, knowing she would already be late, did a quick about-turn, straight into the now on-coming Dr. Charles Preston.

His contempt turned to alarm when he realized the identity of the other party.

"Lady Bridgit! My Lord, I had no idea. Are you hurt? Did I hurt you?" he asked apprehensively, steadying her and assisting her to the nearest bench upon which to sit.

"No, no I am fine, thank you, sir," replied Bridgit, moderately shaken.

As Bridgit regained her composure, she first was struck by the tender strength of the man's hand upon her shoulder, before she realized to whom the hand belonged.

"Dr. Preston," she acknowledged stiffly, straightening her skirt and brushing off her sleeve. He very deliberately removed his now-unwelcome hand from her shoulder.

"Well, you are obviously all right so I will be off. Good day to you, ma'am," he said tersely and with a tip of his head, he left Bridgit to fume.

Well, at least, that was his intention until he saw Bridgit's shawl lying on the pavement. He stood running scenarios through his mind – "do I pretend not to have seen the shawl?" he asked himself then replied, "that would be simplest," he mumbled to himself and started off, only to stop again, "but it is chilly..."

"Blasted woman!" he muttered as he snatched up the shawl and returned to Bridgit who was still seated.

"Yours, I believe, madam," he said curtly and handed her the garment. As she accepted the shawl, their hands touched and even through the soft kid leather of her glove, for a moment Bridgit thought she felt something other than distain from the gentleman and looked up at Dr. Preston. Still seeming shaken and quite alone sitting on the bench, the sight of this attractive woman who had always appeared so strong and wilful but now who looked fragile and abandoned had the effect of softening both his face and the stiffness of his hand.

His countenance now soothed, Dr. Preston uttered caringly and in a low tone, "Don't catch cold. I don't want to have to come and tend to you."

Shocked by this uncharacteristic display of civility, Bridgit allowed her self-protection and cynicism to get the better of her. "I am perfectly capable of tending to myself, thank you, doctor," she replied haughtily.

"Oh, yes, of course you are!" responded the doctor in a rebuffed, sullen and course tone. "Heaven forbid someone should suggest you do anything other than exactly what *you* want to do, even if it is in the interest of protecting you."

Dr. Preston stood soldier-like erect while he gathered his composure then through gritted teeth said, "Good day, madam," and in a highly-controlled manner, stormed off.

"That man!" she scolded herself for again being on the wrong end of an altercation with the pretentious, stubborn, arrogant, pompous, self-important and far too handsome for her own good, Dr. Charles Preston.

Upon arriving home, Bridgit discovered Elizabeth already waiting in the drawing room on the first floor.

"Goodness, what happened to you?" asked Elizabeth, noticing the slight disarray to Bridgit's hair and a small tear in her sleeve as Bridgit kissed her hello.

"Oh, never mind," sighed Bridgit as she sat down next to her friend. "Tell me how your plans are coming along?" she asked, putting a mask of exaggerated brightness over her underlying disturbed demeanour.

Elizabeth was to accompany Lord and Lady Brassey to Australia where Lord Brassey had been appointed Governor of Victoria. Although an explorer when it came to books, science and knowledge in general, Bridgit could not quite get her head around why anyone would want to travel months just to get to what she thought amounted to little more than a colony of convicts at the end of the earth, but for Elizabeth, whose parents had died recently leaving her with name but no fortune, she understood this must have seemed like a wonderful opportunity to start again under the safe tutelage of Lady Brassey.

While Bridgit had her doubts about the merits of the move, she was immensely grateful to her father for arranging the opportunity for their young neighbour. Having met Lady Brassey at the opening of the St Leonard's Pier a few years ago, Bridgit remembered the woman as being kind, refined and gentle, just the right sort of role model for a young, impressionable girl who now found herself alone in the world.

"The 'Sunbeam' is due to set sail in a few weeks and we will apparently arrive in Melbourne sometime in October, all going well," Elizabeth recounted with precision. Having never been to sea, Elizabeth was feeling somewhat apprehensive about the trip, as was Lady Sybil Brassey, whose predecessor had passed away on that very same vessel only a few years earlier.

To ease their respective nerves, Lady Brassey had come up with several statements about the voyage that she and

Elizabeth had rehearsed verbatim to the point they could recite them with vigour and commitment, belying their moderate terror.

Once tales were exhausted of shopping, packing and wondering what style of dresses one wears in Australian society – or even if there was such a thing as 'society' in that far off and relatively uncivilized land of all places, Elizabeth returned home a few doors along Warrior Square to her aunt who had agreed, reluctantly, to stay with the young woman until she set sail.

"Dixon, will you please help me change?" asked Bridgit as she climbed the stairs to her room.

Seeing the tear in her dress, Dixon exclaimed with a slight groan, "Another one, Miss? Mrs. Patterson ain't fixed the brown one yet."

"And you will need to wash this," she said as she handed Dixon the shawl, momentarily thinking back to when her hand touched his...

"Oh, Miss..." sighed the maid when she saw the state of the shawl.

"Just take care of it, please Dixon," said Bridgit with an audible exhale as she undressed.   The   sight   of   the   tear reminded her of that infuriating man and of their first encounter.

It was 1892 and Bridgit had accompanied her father to up to London. Thanks to the train line that now ran from St Leonard's Warrior   Square   to   London   it   was   a relatively easy journey back to the frantic tempo of the modern city, and thankfully just as easy to again leave when one was done. Now used to the relaxed pace of the seaside, Bridgit still wasn't sure how she could once have called London home.

The   pair   were   in   the   city   for   a   gathering at   the   Royal   Institute   on   the   evening   of the fourth of February where a Mr. Nikola Tesla to give a demonstration on the results   of   his   latest   investigations   into electricity.

Sir Frank Darnell held a fascination for all things   scientific   and   all   conversations surrounding such a subject; in particular, those mental sojourns that encourage one to leave behind what is oft referred to as 'common   sense'   and   challenge   one's assumptions   of   what   is   possible.   This captivation   he   had   passed   on   to   his daughter.

Indeed, on the very day Bridgit was born on the eighth of December, 1864, Sir Frank was in attendance with his fellow members of the Royal Society at the rather crowded Somerset House for the reading of James Clerk Maxwell's paper spelling out the as before unknown laws of electromagnetism, laws that Tesla was about to demonstrate; and laws that would soon impact Bridgit in ways she could never have expected.

As they settled into their seats, Sir Frank acknowledged with a nod the gentleman sitting to Bridgit's right, just as Tesla started to speak.

In a softly-spoken, rather high-pitched accented voice, he began: "I cannot find words to express how deeply I feel the honour of addressing some of the foremost thinkers of the present time, and so many able scientific men, engineers and electricians, of the country greatest in scientific achievements. The results which I have the honour to present before such a gathering I cannot call my own. There are among you not a few who can lay better claim than myself on any feature of merit which this work may contain."

After a short introductory as to the theory that led him up to his new line of work, Mr. Tesla began his experimental demonstrations and the crowd were captivated until the lecturer dealt with the possibility of transmitting electricity without wires, at which point the man beside Bridgit scoffed, not rowdily but loud enough to bring frowns and shushes from those near him, and a very stern look from Bridgit. A look that was returned with a matching and decidedly severe glare from Preston.

"But such cables will not be constructed, for ere long intelligence—transmitted without wires—will throb through the earth like a pulse through a living organism," Tesla continued. "The wonder is that, with the present state of knowledge and the experiences gained, no attempt is being made to disturb the electrostatic or magnetic condition of the earth, and transmit, if nothing else, intelligence."

Once the demonstration was over and people were leaving the auditorium, Sir Frank walked over and shook hands with the gentleman in question.

"Dr. Preston, I would like to introduce my daughter, Lady Bridgit Darnell. Bridgit, this is my esteemed colleague, Dr. Charles Preston," said Sir Frank as he presented his daughter.

"Charmed," Preston said abruptly, giving Bridgit a quick glance from toe to head before turning his attention back to her father.

"What did you make of all that, Sir Frank?" asked Preston, having already made up his own mind that, while he agreed with the general science of electricity, he was yet to be convinced that it was a benign means of power.

"I think it is fascinating," interjected Bridgit, forcing her way into the conversation more to annoy the arrogant gentleman than a wish to engage with him.

"And I suppose you believe this all to be perfectly safe, do you?" he asked Bridgit with a condescending tone.

"Mr. Tesla didn't seem to think there was an issue," she replied assuredly, having just seen the successful demonstrations for herself and feeling on very sure ground.

Preston took a piece of paper from his coat pocket and began to read, "On the first application of the process to the face, the jaws of the deceased criminal began to quiver, and the adjoining muscles were horribly contorted, and one eye was actually opened. In the subsequent part of the process the right hand was raised and clenched, and the legs and thighs were set in motion."

Both Sir Frank and Bridgit looked at him with curiosity and horror.

"Do you know what this is from?" asked Preston as he held aloft the paper. "It is an extract from the Newgate Calendar discussing in great detail the use of Mr. Telsla's electricity on a dead man. A dead man! Not only that, but a dead man who was found guilty of murdering his wife and child by drowning them in the Paddington Canal and then hanged as a result. Now, while I am sure there are many wonderful and practical uses for such a tool, the fact that it potentially has the power to bring someone back to life... I am a doctor, but that, my friends, is the realm of God and I want no part of it," he continued.

"These carnival-like exhibitions by Tesla make it seem as though electricity is a harmless toy with which we can play, and it may be 'fascinating' as you put it, Lady Bridgit," he said with mockery, "but while I have no doubt it will become part of our lives in ways today we cannot even fathom, the application of this force will also come at significant cost to life and peace of mind."

Bridgit became aware that her eyebrows were raised so high her forehead was beginning to hurt as she listened to the diatribe that, when over, was followed by all three becoming quite uncomfortably taciturn.

"Well, we must be off," said Sir Frank, breaking the awkward silence that had enveloped the trio. "Good to see you, Preston," as he tipped his head to the doctor.

"Lady Bridgit," Dr. Preston's clipped tone as he took her gloved hand to bid her goodnight left Bridgit cold, but then, just as he released her grasp, his eyes caught hers for slightly longer than cordial and in them, she saw... Well, she wasn't sure what she saw, but it left her slightly breathless.

"Come along, Bridgit," said Sir Frank and motioned to his daughter with a hand behind her waist, guiding her through the doorway

Lost in thought after their encounter, Bridgit wasn't paying attention as they entered the carriage and caught her shoe in the hem of her dress, causing a minor tear.

"What a horrid man," Bridgit said to her father when they were settled.

"You do him an injustice, my dear," replied Sir Frank. "Dr. Preston may be abrupt at times, but he is passionate about his work and one of the finest doctors I have ever come across. What he doesn't know about the advances in medicine, and indeed in much of modern science, is not worth knowing."

Bridgit pondered on this, not quite sure she and her father were talking about the same man.

"He's still a horrid man," Bridgit muttered as Dixon helped her off with her dress.

"What's that, Miss?" asked Dixon.

"Oh, nothing. Never mind, Dixon," sighed Bridgit.

Bridgit had not been at home when the package was delivered and it was not until just before supper did she even notice its arrival.

Wrapped in brown paper and tied with string, the package was addressed to 'Lady Bridgit Darnell, Warrior Square, St Leonard's-On-Sea', and the return address was noted simply as 'Lynton, 143 Maybury Road, Woking'.

"Bertie!" she exclaimed as she hurriedly opened first the letter that accompanied the package.

My Dearest Friend,

As you may know, Isabel and I have divorced and it is my delight to tell you, my dear, that I have married a wonderful girl.

Jane and I are perfectly happy and I feel this year will be the turning point in my life.

Enclosed, please find one of the first copies of my time machine book. It seems a long time since we discussed the possibility of such a contraption while hiding out from my mother at Uppark! Those were the days.

As you will see, they had a challenge with my name in this edition, but I am assured it will be corrected if there is indeed a second printing. One can only hope.

I trust all is well with you. Do come and visit with us soon.

Your truest friend,

Bertie

As soon as Bridgit saw the cover, she immediately sank into the seat that thankfully was beneath her.

Her 'dream' came flooding back in waves that felt as though they would drown her.

"They didn't even get his name right at first," the man had said in her dream – and now here she was, holding a book that he not only divulged would be published, but with the author listed on the cover as H.S. Wells instead of H.G. Wells, just as he had foretold!

"Bridgit, darling, you are as white as a sheet," her father said with alarm as he entered the room and hastily went to his daughter's side. "What's wrong? Are you unwell?" Seeing the letter, he asked, "Is it bad news?"

Bridgit sat motionless for the longest time and when she did speak, it was in slow, halting phrases.

"Papa, I need your help," she started.

"Anything, darling. Is there some kind of trouble?" he asked with concerned agitation as he sat down on the couch beside her.

As best as she was able, Bridgit recounted the dream to her father and with as much detail as she could recite. Upon finishing, she passed the book to him, saying, "and then this..."

Sir Frank sat and stared at the book for what to Bridgit felt like an eternity before he rose, walking slowly and methodically to the other end of the room and back again, placing the book on a table near the window.

"Have you mentioned this to anyone else?" he asked.

"Not a soul, Papa. Until today I thought it was only a very strange dream," she replied as she felt for her mother's chatelaine on her waistband.

Sir Frank was a man of science, a member of both the Royal Society and the Royal Institution, but even he was perplexed by the notions and detail in Bridgit's recital.

Bridgit sat motionless, watching her father's internal ponderings reflected on his face in slight twitches and eyebrow-lifts as his eyes moved about the room, focusing nowhere but inwardly on his thoughts.

Finally, he said, "I have a question to which I would like you to give serious consideration before you answer, my darling, as it may have significant consequences." He paused and Bridgit straightened her back, lifting her head slightly, ready for the query.

"You said this man came to visit you in your dream, and told you all about how he has been able to travel through time, and he had your mother's chatelaine," his voice went up at the end making it sound like a question, to which Bridgit nodded, and again touched the object in question. He continued, "so my question, darling girl, is – did he travel to visit you as you suggested, or did he somehow come across your mother's chatelaine in the future, and you travelled through time to visit him?"

It had been more than a week since Bridgit confided in her father the details of her 'dream' and although they had briefly discussed it from time to time, he continually suggested he was 'looking into it' and they would discuss it later – but 'later' had not yet arrived..

What Bridgit didn't know, was that her father had chosen Dr. Preston of all people with whom to share the details of her adventure and the two men had been busy ever since evaluating as best they could the science and plausibility of what Markus had to say.

What Bridgit also did not know was that on the very day she shared the details of the 'dream' with her father, Sir Frank was about to have one of the most difficult conversations of his life with his daughter. Dr. Preston and Sir Frank had become close not only because they were colleagues who had similar interests, but because, as Sir Frank's doctor, Dr. Preston was treating him for what they now knew to be a terminal illness.

Two weeks later found Sir Frank and Dr. Preston again meeting in the library.

"I just couldn't tell her," disclosed Sir Frank to his friend and confidante as he leaned with resignation against the mantle of the marble fireplace. "Preston, if there really is something to this time-travel notion, I would rather spend what time I have left investigating it than to have her fussing about me and demanding I take it easy and rest."

Dr. Preston nodded. An intense sadness had befallen his countenance at the knowledge that he would not only soon lose his best friend, but also that Bridgit would then be without both her parents; essentially alone in the world.

"If there is the slightest chance she could go back and know her mother," Sir Frank said, his eyes glistening and a pleading in his voice. "Or that she and I could be reunited..."

Dr. Preston walked over to the distressed gentleman and placed a comforting hand on his shoulder.

"We will do all we can," the doctor said softly, wishing he also meant there was something more to be done for Sir Frank's condition.

"All right, let's get back to work," said Sir Frank, straightening his back, lifting his chin and giving a veiled smile and nod to Dr. Preston. "Did you hear anything yet about that Morgan Robertson chap? He seems to be our best bet so far since everything else the dream-fellow mentioned is decades away from even happening just yet."

"We haven't definitively heard news about Robertson," replied Dr. Preston. "but Anthony Barrow, you know him, the artistic fellow at the Club that is always wearing odd-coloured socks. It seems Barrow met a writer called Morgan Robertson in New York recently and this could be the same man but since he hasn't yet published – or perhaps even written – the book about the sinking of the Titanic ship, there is no real way of knowing for sure. We certainly didn't find any Morgan Robertsons here in London that could be him."

"If only I could still be here in the coming years to see for myself if things Bridgit's 'dream man' mentioned come to pass. I scarcely see any other way of proving this whole thing wasn't in fact just an elaborate dream – but then there is the book!" Sir Frank said as he picked up H.G. Wells' novel from the mahogany desk.

"I know Wells and Bridgit have been friends since childhood, but there is no way they could have concocted this as a scheme. I mean, they did get up to some mischief when they were young, but Bridgit was much too upset for it all to be a joke," Sir Frank continued.

"We have been going back and forth for days and days over the notes you and Lady Bridgit took about the episode, my friend," said Preston. "Everything except that book," he pointed to the "Time Machine" novel, "is still apparently in the future – or more precisely in *some possible* future. There are many elements that I find intriguing, but without knowing more, or being able to talk to one of the scientists – who haven't yet been born... What a mess!"

Sir Frank nodded his concurrence and as he appeared to be about to say something, he paused... It seemed to the doctor as though time slowed to a crawl as he watched Sir Frank close his eyes... put his palm to his forehead... and collapse in what appeared to be a lifeless form. In the process, the decanter on the nearby table was knocked onto the floor.

Seeing Sir Frank lying motionless on the floor, Preston would later chide himself that his first thought was, "How do I tell Bridgit..?" before he hastened to the side of his friend.

"Good Lord, man," said Dr. Preston as he saw Sir Frank's eyes open. "You can't go kicking the bucket on me yet. We still have too much work to do." He smiled at Sir Frank's acknowledgement of his comment, reassured that his friend was still with him – at least for a little while longer.

"Well, that was a bit inconvenient," said Sir Frank as he came to and saw the upended decanter. "Dixon will never let me hear the end of this," he laughed as he weakly pointed to the stain on the carpet.

Helping him to the chair, Dr. Preston added, "she is a bit of a tyrant, that one."

Dr. Preston went to take Sir Frank's pulse only to have his hand gently brushed aside by the patient.

"I'm all right, Preston. Well, as all right as I can be given the circumstances," he smiled sadly and continued. "Will you do something for me?" he asked then chuckled, "Goodness! I should say, will you do something *else* for me?"

Both men smiled.

From his pocket, Sir Frank took a small, leather-bound, well-worn book and handed it to Dr. Preston.

"Make sure she gets this, will you?" he implored the doctor. "It's funny, until now there has always been a Darnell son to pass it on to. Someone who would carry on the name and the family heritage. But anyway, Bridgit will hopefully to marry one day..." his voice trailed off as he looked at Dr. Preston and smiled his intent and blessing. Should indeed the occasion arise when he was no longer around to give his permission in person, Sir Frank wanted to be sure his wishes were understood.

"She has no idea how you feel about her, you know," smiled the kindly father, "but despite her protestations, I am quite convinced she feels the same about you – even if she has not yet acknowledged it anyone, let alone to herself."

"But..." Dr. Preston's protestations were silenced by Sir Frank's interjection.

"When the time comes, just give it to her, tell her I am sorry to have left her... Tell her I love her more than there are words to express... Tell her I hope to see her again... perhaps... and whatever else happens, happens," said Sir Frank. "Perhaps she can use it to find me in some alternate universe where I am not dead – and if not, at least she has something by which to remember me, and verse to comfort her as it comforted me after her mother passed away."

The book in question was a small, pocket-sized copy of the Bible, and printed by Evan Tyler over two-hundred years earlier.

As he examined the object he knew to be so dear to his friend, Dr. Preston went to open it and stopped, asking, "do you mind?"

"Of course not," was the kindly reply and Sir Frank gestured his approval.

The book was reverently opened by the doctor and gently he turned page after page, as though looking for something in particular, and ignoring the slight red ribbon that marked a different place within. Finding his intended place, Preston began to read from the Book of

Psalms, "Commit thy way unto the Lord; trust in Him, and He shall bring it to pass."

Dr. Preston looked at his friend who was now starting to regain some colour. "Let us just pray that whatever happens, it will all turn out for the best."

"Thank you," said Sir Frank as he took Dr. Preston's hand in his right and patted the connection with his left, before wrapping his fingers around the union.

"I will take care of her," acknowledged Dr. Preston, then added with a curious smile, "if she lets me!" Both men laughed, conceding the rather stubborn nature of Lady Bridgit Darnell.

It was a fine day as Bridgit bid farewell to her young friend, Elizabeth.

"I want you to have this," said Elizabeth, giving a small, finely and very distinguishably detailed gold cross on a delicate chain to Bridgit. "It was hand-engraved to match this one," she continued, holding the one that hung around her own neck out for display. When I was born, my father bought two identical crosses, one for me and one for my mother." Bridgit nodded as she studied the cross in her hand. "You have been the closest thing to a sister I have ever known," said Elizabeth, with tears brimming in her eyes. "I am now wearing the one my mother wore all my life and I would like you to have mine. My parents adored you and I am sure they would want you to have it."

Clutching the memento in her hand, Bridgit wrapped her arms around her young friend, holding her tight, and whispering through her tears, "Take care of yourself, and know that if ever you need me, all you need to do is find a way to contact me and I will do whatever I can to make sure you are all right. Just think of me as though I am already there, and you will never be alone." At which time, Elizabeth's aunt signalled it was the moment to leave.

"Take care of yourself, too," Elizabeth cried as the two released their embrace.

Bridgit watched as the carriage drove to the end of the Square until it turned right along the seafront, out of sight.

"She will be sorely missed," said Sir Frank, walking back inside with his daughter.

"Yes, she will," agreed Bridgit, as she fastened the cross around her neck.

At that moment, a visitor arrived.

"Dr. Preston! What are you doing here?" asked Bridgit, not sure whether she was delighted or annoyed at the visit.

"I am here to see your father," he replied with a nod to his friend and colleague.

"Again? Oh, I see," she said and, rather than be on the end of yet another altercation with the good doctor, she bid her leave. "Then, you will excuse me," she responded and walked inside, up the stairs to her room to change her dress before calling on a beloved friend; an Irish woman of means who decades ago had moved with her husband to England. Whenever she saw Bridgit, the dowager related her delight at the fact Bridgit's parents saw fit to keep part of the girl's Irish heritage in her name.

Sir Frank's mother's name was Bridgette, being one generation removed from French heritage, but only two before that back to English.

Lady Mary's mother's name was Maud, but her maternal grandmother's name was a very Irish, Brigid.

Upon Bridgit's birth, there was much discussion about what she would be called but, thankfully as far as Bridgit was concerned, her parents decided upon an amalgam of Bridgette and Brigid, being Bridgit.

"I often ponder what life would have been like as a "Maud"," Bridgit mused.

After arriving home and amusing herself for several hours, admittedly frustrated at not knowing what the two men found so fascinating and time-consuming on such a regular occurrence of late, Bridgit entered the library.

"Excuse me. Mr. Chapman is wondering whether Dr. Preston will be staying for dinner, Papa?" asked Bridgit, now attired in a stunning gold satin dress.

"Yes! Of course, you must," Sir Frank motioned to Dr. Preston and without waiting for a reply to his daughter's question. "Tell Mr. Chapman to have another place set and Mrs. Patterson to make sure she has something special for our guest. Perhaps she might even see if the Monsieur is up to creating some of his magic for us?"

Bridgit looked at Dr. Preston who simply smiled and nodded his compliance.

"I'm not dressed for dinner, Sir Frank," Dr. Preston protested, knowing that his objection would fall on deaf ears.

"Oh, don't worry about all that," was the reply. "I won't change, either if it will make you feel any better. Come, let's put a bee in Chapman's bonnet and have a drink before dinner. Bridgit, will you join us?"

"If Dr. Preston doesn't mind my intrusion," she said with slight acerbity.

"Not at all. He wouldn't mind a bit," said Sir Frank jovially, taking his daughter by the arm and leading her into the drawing room, with Dr. Preston following behind.

Dinner was a lively affair and the combination of Monsieur Dubois' flair with Mrs. Patterson's support delivered several elegant and delicious courses on such short notice that Bridgit was certain neither her blue nor her brown dress would be mended any time soon as if asked about them, Mrs. Patterson would go into a great discourse on how she only had just so much time in the day and yet she was expected to produce 'loaves and fishes' miracles just because some fancy doctor comes to visit... "Where was she supposed to find the extra time to mend dresses?" she would ask... Bridgit thought it best to simply order another when next she went to town.

After the final course had been consumed, Bridgit rose, saying, "well, gentlemen, if you will excuse me..."

Both Sir Frank and Dr. Preston came to their feet as Bridgit stood up, but almost immediately, Sir Frank fell back into his chair, his face ashen.

"Papa!" cried Bridgit as she raced to his side.

Dr. Preston had already tipped back Sir Frank's head and was checking his pulse.

"Get me a cloth and some cold water! Immediately!" yelled the doctor.

Hearing the commotion, Mr. Chapman had entered the room just in time to hear the command and motioned to Bridgit that he would take care of it.

"Papa... Can you hear me?" she said as she patted his hand, fitfully, kneeling beside her father.

"Please! Give me some room," commanded Dr. Preston and Bridgit took several hesitant steps backward.

He felt for a pulse in one wrist... then the other... then the neck...

He opened one of Sir Frank's eyelids, then the other...

He held the back of a spoon up to Sir Frank's mouth to check for any sign of breath...

When Mr. Chapman returned with the cloth and cold water, Dr. Preston simply waved him away with a saddened look.

It took a moment for Bridgit to realize what had just transpired between Preston and Chapman but, looking back and forth between the two, the gravity and reality of the situation set in with a mighty blow.

"Nooooooooooo!" cried Bridgit, racing back to her father's side, only to be caught by Dr. Preston.

"Let me GO!" demanded Bridgit as she attempted to squirrel out of Dr. Preston's grasp.

"Get Dixon," demanded Dr. Preston, not knowing how else to calm the hysterical outburst.

As Dixon rushed into the room, saying "Mr. Chapman said it was urge..." She didn't finish the word, let alone the sentence, when her eyes met Dr. Preston's and were then directed to the now deceased Sir Frank Darnell.

Mrs. Dixon nodded her understanding to the doctor and helped him usher Bridgit from the room and upstairs to her bedchamber.

The cabinet-maker on Norman Road, due to the quality of his workmanship in the construction of coffins, had been requested to manufacture the casket and to see to the transportation of Sir Frank's body from the house to the church on the day of the funeral.

Bridgit was astonished to see so many people gathered outside their Warrior Square home as the casket was carried, head-first, from the building.

As she stood on the landing, black crape tied with ribbon affixed upon the door behind her, and watched the men take the box containing her father's body down the steps across the pavement and to the waiting carriage, Bridgit marvelled at the almost wave-like motion of men removing their hats and caps, one after the next after the next after the next...

Normally a hive of activity, it seemed today as though not even a seagull chose to disrupt the silent reverence that had descended upon the Square – or was it just that her faculty of hearing had, like her other senses, reached its limit and could absorb no more?

Bridgit felt an arm steady her as she navigated the steps down from the house and at first she thought it was her father... When she looked up, she was both saddened and comforted to see that it was Dr. Preston providing the strength, reassurance and support – the role her father had always adopted – until now...

Preston would normally have been a pall-bearer for his best-friend, however in this instance, he felt he was of best service beside his friend's only offspring.

The procession progressed on foot behind the carriage, along the seafront and to the church. Bridgit did not want to exclude any of the working-class men and women whom her father had so respected for their hard-work and diligence in their individual contribution to the local community he so adored. As such, she dispensed with tradition and merely placed an announcement in the Hastings Observer, asking all who esteemed and admired her father to pay their respects.

It seemed to Bridgit as though the entire populations of St Leonard's and Hastings had come out to honour her father's passing.

The rest of the day was a series of one vague image smeared into the next, like an impressionist or sfumato painting gone inextricably wrong.

Finally, Bridgit found herself being tucked up into bed by an unusually quiet Dixon who, Bridgit observed, simply went about her activities and without uttering a single word, left Bridgit alone in her in the middle of her double four-post mahogany bed – alone with her thoughts; alone in a large, empty house that, aside from the servants who slept up on the fourth floor, was now home to no one but her, not even a pet; alone to stare into the single, solitary flame contained in the lamp placed beside her bed; and alone to face an unknown future for which she felt completely unprepared.

Six weeks had passed since the funeral and although Dr. Preston called daily to check on Bridgit, he had not yet given her the gift entrusted to him by Sir Frank, knowing that as soon as he did, there would be a barrage of questions of which he was dreading. However, the time came when he could put it off no longer.

Seated in the sunlit morning room, Dr. Preston rose as Bridgit entered.

"Lady Bridgit," he said with a smile.

"Dr. Preston," she replied pleasantly, although looking and sounding tired through to the core. "What brings you out so early this morning?"

Dr. Preston's character was such that he could never have been accused as a coward, but his inner voices were certainly leaning toward cowardice as his thoughts went from, 'perhaps I will give it to her another day,' to 'she doesn't look well enough just yet,' to 'maybe I will just leave it behind when I leave and not say anything...'

"Will you please be seated? I have something to discuss with you," he motioned Bridgit to the chair beside the window.

He carefully placed Sir Frank's bible on the small table beside Bridgit and took a step back, saying nothing.

Puzzled, Bridgit looked at the book, then to Dr. Preston, then back to the book before saying with confusion in her tone, "that is my father's bible," as she picked up the object in question.

Dr. Preston still said nothing as Bridgit opened the slim red ribbon used as a bookmark by her father and read the passage he had marked for her: Psalm 73:26 "My flesh and my heart may fail, but God is the strength of my heart and my portion forever."

"I don't understand," said Bridgit tentatively with apprehension, confusion and pain clutching at her stomach and throat. "Why do you have my father's bible?" She stared at Preston.

"He gave it to me to give to you," replied Dr. Preston, "and he said to tell you he is sorry to have left you, that he loves you more than words can express, and that..." Dr. Preston paused, making sure he recited his friend's message as faithfully as possible.

"Go on," Bridgit instructed.

"That he hopes to see you again one day, perhaps..." Preston concluded feeling relieved he had told her but now painfully aware of the onslaught that was sure to follow.

"I still don't understand," said Bridgit, now more perplexed than before. "How could my father have told you he was sorry to leave me?"

Preston was hoping that a gaping abyss would appear beneath his feet at that moment and swallow him whole – even that would be preferable to telling Bridgit that he had known her father was dying and didn't divulge the secret to her.

Since no chasms manifested to whisk him away, Dr. Preston had no choice but to continue.

"Your father knew he only had a limited time and he wanted to investigate as much as he could the possibility that one really could travel through time and different realities. He hoped that not only might you and he be reunited, but that you could meet your mother," said Preston, not sure if any of this now made sense even to him, let alone to Bridgit.

"You knew..." Her quiet monotone belied the scathing accusation in her eyes.

"There was nothing that could be done, Bridgit. He didn't want you fussing,"

"Fussing!" Bridgit exclaimed with fury. "My father was dying and you admit you didn't have the common decency to tell me! What kind of gentlemen are you?" She didn't wait for a reply. "Get out!" she screamed pushing all lady-like composure aside, clutching the bible to her chest, turning her back on the doctor and doing her best to breathe through the convulsions of rage and gut-wrenching despair.

He left without uttering another word and spent the entire day walking along the seafront, pondering how much, in the space of only a few short months his life had completely changed.

He had gone from being one who liked most his own company and that of his books, to one who was happiest in the company of his best friend – a friend who had now departed leaving a hole in his heart that felt palpable.

He had gone from being a self-proclaimed bachelor, to having such deep and profound feelings for a particular woman, that every day was filled with thoughts of her, worries about her, and notions of how to bring a smile back to her face – and yet now his admission had been so injurious to her, that same woman wanted nothing to do with him, and that was a hole he felt sucked the very breath from his lungs, the strength from his legs, and the will from his being.

Unable to walk no further, Dr. Charles Preston sat on a nearby bench and watched the sun sink into the horizon across the English Channel, his hopes for his future sinking with it.

Chapter Eight - The Ring

A packet was delivered by messenger early in the morning two days hence and Bridgit, noting the sender, was in two minds about whether or not to even open it, but curiosity had the better of her. That and, although she had not forgiven the doctor, she still found it baffling she should have the slightest interest in what he would have to say – but she did.

The note read:

My dearest Lady Bridgit,

While I would do anything in my power to remove the hurt you have suffered first at the loss of your father, and second at discovering he knew his passing was imminent, I can not apologize for keeping that knowledge from you.

Your father was my most cherished friend and it was his wish to spare you as much as possible, and that also was, and is my wish.

From the moment you entrusted the contents of your dream to Sir Frank, he and I spent countless hours investigating whether there was in fact something to the notion of time travel.

Knowing he did not have long to live, your father deeply desired that if there was the slightest chance you and he could be reunited after his passing, or indeed if you might meet and get to know your mother – if there was the slightest chance, he wanted you to have that – and so do I.

...but I also want you to find your way back home.

As such, I enclose my great-grandmother's posy ring, given to her by my great-grandfather and passed down eventually to my mother who, like yours, died when I was but an infant.

If you do decide to experiment for yourself – which, knowing you, I am certain you will, despite my wishes to the contrary – please take this ring with you. You seem to have an aversion to people looking out for you and doing what they can to protect you but – if the fellow in your dream was correct and that not only does this time travel notion actually work, but that you need to have a connection to an object to keep you grounded, please keep this ring with you.

Short of testing it for ourselves, your father and I were unable to prove nor disprove the time travel theory but if you do in fact manage it, please make sure you know how to come back - please - and I am not a man to beg, so read into that what you will.

I understand you do not wish to see me, but know I give this ring to you with my utmost respect and devotion, and the hopes that the inscription contained therein will one day bring pleasant recollections.

Yours,

Charles Preston

Bridgit carefully unfurled the piece of velvet cloth to find within a delicate, plain gold posy ring. The inscription inside the band read,

"When this ye see, remember me."

"Papa," she cried as she sank into a chair, holding the note in one hand and the ring in the other.

"I don't know what to do, Papa!" Bridgit had never felt so totally and utterly lost and floundering.

Although her mother had died when she was a baby, her father's strength and love had always guided her. If ever she felt unsteady, she would seek his counsel and soon after regain her bearings.

Even when, as a young woman of twenty-one she had developed great depth of feeling for – and all expected her to marry – a tall, gallant fellow who was to tragically die in a riding accident before any formal understanding was entered into. Still Bridgit eventually rallied back to her usual positive and cheerful self.

Now she felt she had nothing.

An empty house.

An empty life.

...and a heart that was so broken she scarcely dare breathe for fear she would disturb the fragments and stir up memories – or worse, hopes – hopes of a future, or futures, that were now impossible.

...or were they..?

For the first time in months, Bridgit felt she had a direction, a mission.

Going to her father's study, Bridgit fossicked around until she found the detailed notes she had written on her dream – and she was surprised to see the additional notes written by Dr. Preston and her father's own hand during their analysis and discussion.

Putting the entire set of pages into a leather folio, Bridgit went up to the drawing room and set herself to the task of immersing into every minute detail of the dream, every word, every element she could recall.

It was mid-afternoon by the time the staff decided someone should intervene. "Miss, you must have something to eat," said a concerned Dixon after entering the room and seeing it in such disarray.

"Mrs. Chapman can make you up a tray," she continued, pleading encouragingly.

"Thank you, Dixon," said Bridgit without looking up from the documents in her hand. "I am fine. Please just leave me."

There was an extended silence. Dixon hadn't moved.

Bridgit looked up from her papers into the eyes of her faithful servant.

"Truly, Dixon," she said with sincerity and almost an apology, "I really am fine. Thank you for taking such good care of me."

"As you will, Miss. And it ain't easy taking care of you but I do my level best," Dixon smiled at Bridgit as she turned and left the young woman to her endeavours.

"All right, Papa," Bridgit said aloud as though seeking her father's counsel. "As far as I can tell, I need to have some item of personal resonance for where I want to go. Let's start with that."

Bridgit reached through the slit in her skirt to take her father's bible from the pocket in her petticoat, and placed it on the table.

"That's that," she said with conviction, and then stopped. "No, wait," she uttered as she removed her mother's chatelaine from her waist and placed it beside the bible.

Bridgit stood staring at the objects before reaching back into her pocket and removing the ring Dr. Preston had given her.

Holding it between her thumb and forefinger, Bridgit sat down in contemplation.

"What should I do, Papa?" she said, hoping in vain for an intelligent reply however she wasn't even really sure what her question meant.

'What should I do?' Did that concern whether or not she should attempt to reconnect through time with her father, or even her mother? Or, did it relate to whether or not she should find out if Charles Preston had intentions toward her?

It crossed Bridgit's mind to reach out to Bertie Wells for his input on her situation, but she felt an urgency to take action that would prohibit any traditional means of communication, and there was no guarantee he would be able to help, even if he could be reached.

So, now Bridgit had three items for the personal resonance part of the equation.

"So, what's next?" Bridgit asked aloud.

Even though she understood many of the other elements that were shared with her in her dream, there were two factors that still concerned her.

First, she wasn't sure whether Markus had shared all the steps with her and so there was an element of uncertainty as to whether this would work.

The second was his warning, "you have to follow exactly what I tell you to do, or you won't be able to come back to the same time and place you left." Only, he didn't get around to telling her what it was she needed to do!

"So, it looks like unless I can find the man from my dream, I won't be coming back," said Bridgit aloud and very hesitatingly as she looked around the room and then picked up Dr. Preston's ring.

'When this ye see, remember me' – she read the engraving and spoke to the ring, "You certainly have complicated matters."

After what felt like an eon, darkness eventually fell that evening over St

Leonards-On-Sea and, following a light supper, Bridgit retired early.

"Thank you for absolutely everything," Bridgit gave Dixon an unexpected hug.

"You're very welcome, Miss," said Dixon, a little taken aback. "It's a pleasure. Now get into bed and I'll be sure to make sure Mrs. Chapman fixes you something special for breakfast. You need to keep up your strength."

"Thank you, Dixon," Bridgit smiled as Dixon left the room, closing the door behind her, and Bridgit secretly hoping she would not be here for breakfast – well, at least not in this reality with this consciousness.

"Hmm, if this does work," she spoke to herself, "does that mean there will be another me eating Mrs. Chapman's breakfast? What a curious thought..."

Sitting up in bed, Bridgit unfurled the large handkerchief once belonging to her father in which she had placed the bible, the chatelaine and the ring.

The three items lay on her lap and she wished that any one of the three could tell her what to do at this moment.

Not receiving any such guidance, Bridgit gently lifted the item that was so precious to Charles and placed it on the ring finger of her right hand. The other two, she carefully re-wrapped in the handkerchief and clutched her fingers around the precious package.

"I am not sure in what order to do all this, or even if I know for certain *what* to do," Bridgit thought to herself, "but here goes..."

Bridgit extinguished the lamp beside her bed, cuddled up under the covers, and clutched her treasured parcel to her breast. Feeling a combination of excitement, apprehension, curiosity, concern and unfortunately an underlying deep anxiety, she began to follow the rest of Markus' instructions and then drifted into the dreaming state...

Bridgit awoke to find herself clinging to a life-preserver, the water thick with oil. Screams and hollow cries filled the air and the salt water seemed to shower her from both above and below as what she would later learn were German planes made several passes, strafing those bobbing about in the pandemonium, their bullets whizzing past and creating a bloody spray as they hit the water.

Somehow, she found herself in the worst maritime disaster in British history – a disaster that occurred during World War II (and that Churchill refused to allow the news outlets to cover for fear of a further drop in morale). In that one single incident as many men, women and children died as in the Titanic and 9/11 disasters *combined...*

...and that, my Friends, is where you find Bridgit in Book Two...

If you would like me to email you when the next book is published, simply go to www.QuantumLace.com and give me your email address.

I hope you have loved reading Bridgit's story as much as I have loved researching and writing it...

See you in the next Quantum Lace Book!

~ *Bella*

PS: if you would be so kind as to leave a review, I would very much appreciate it.

Thank you!

Acknowledgements & Thanks

It is always a tricky endeavour to thank people because there is always the tendency to forget someone!

So, first of all, anyone I haven't mentioned below – **thank you!** :-)

I would like to acknowledge and thank (not in any particular order):

- All the quantum physicists, historians, authors, presenters, researchers, seekers and others who have provided (and continue to provide in many cases) me with insights, knowledge and inspiration.

- Mr. Walter Van Dyk, my dear Friend whose glorious Victorian home I leased while writing this book – and if you look at the cover, the patterning that appears as a watermark is actually a photograph I took of the panelling on the walls of the home; and the spine on the artwork is actually a graphic from a photograph I took of the ceiling lace-work in that same home that inspired the title, 'Quantum Lace' –

when I created the cover art, I wanted to include elements that contributed to the book.

- Aldo, Franco and all the Family at La Bella Vista in St Leonards-On-Sea, UK where I would sit outside for hours at a time enjoying delicious food, wine, and fabulous company while undertaking the rest of the research that made this book possible.

- Jo, Scott and all the staff at my 'writing pub', Ye Olde Pumphouse in Hastings, UK where I wrote the vast majority of this book.

- Ms. Laura Klemm for her feedback and all important 'glass' of tea.

- Ms. Megan Mathis for everything...

- All my dear Friends (you know who you are) for your love and support, many of whom have put up with my questions, and being asked to read snippets of Bridgit's adventures as the book came together.

- Mr. T.J. Tauriello for all your public relations assistance in promoting Bridgit and her story.

- My Facebook Family for your love and encouragement.

- Mr. Julian Fellowes, my role model in so many ways, whose work is elegant, heart-warming and inspiring and who sets the benchmark of quality to which I aspire.

- The wonderful people of Hastings and St Leonards-On-Sea – and the organisations who promote and support them – who welcomed me so warmly. I have made friendships here that will last a lifetime.

- National Trust and English Heritage, and all who work for and support these organisations who have provided a wealth of information and who help preserve the buildings and history that I so adore. I am honoured to be a Member of both.

- Mrs. Gillian Fazan whose lovely Georgian apartment I leased at the time of publication of this book, overlooking the magnificent Torquay Harbour.

- AirBnB (and their wonderful Team!) who make it possible for me to lease unique and often historic properties all over the world...

- ...and everyone who loves to read and write books... You are the ones who keep Bridgit alive...

Thank you...

...and remember, if you would like me to email you when the next book is published, simply go to www.QuantumLace.com and provide me with your email address.

Well, it is time to head off to the next location in my world travels as a Luxurious Nomad and to find another perfect 'writing pub' for Bridgit's next book.

Until then, sending love and smiles to all...

Bella St John

CPSIA information can be obtained
at www.ICGtesting.com
Printed in the USA
LVOW11s2027020317
525958LV00001B/84/P